Dragon

LIONEL
and the Book of
BEASTS

LIONEL
and the Book of
BEASTS

by E. Nesbit

Retold and Illustrated by Michael Hague

▤ HarperCollins*Publishers*

Lionel and the Book of Beasts
Illustrations copyright © 2006 by Michael Hague
Manufactured in China.

Library of Congress Cataloging-in-Publication Data
Nesbit, E. (Edith), 1858–1924
[Book of beasts]
Lionel and the book of beasts / by E. Nesbit ; retold and illustrated by Michael
Hague.— 1st ed.
p.   cm.
Summary: As young King Lionel turns the pages of his magical book,
a hungry red dragon and other creatures in the illustrations come to life.
ISBN-10: 0-688-14006-8 — ISBN-10: 0-06-084272-5 (lib. bdg.)
ISBN-13: 978-0-688-14006-9 — ISBN-13: 978-0-06-084272-7 (lib. bdg.)
[1. Fairy tales. 2. Kings, queens, rulers, etc.—Fiction. 3. Dragons—Fiction.
4. Books and reading—Fiction. 5. Magic—Fiction.] I. Hague, Michael, ill. II. Title.
PZ8.N365Lio 2006   2005002807
[Fic]—dc22

Typography by Jeanne L. Hogle
1 2 3 4 5 6 7 8 9 10
❖
First Edition

To the one I love

Lionel was building a palace with his blocks when the news came.

Nurse came in and said, "Master Lionel, dear, they've come to fetch you to go and be King."

In the drawing room were two very grave-looking gentlemen in red robes and gold coronets. They bowed low to Lionel, and the gravest one said, "Sire, your great-great-great-great-great-grandfather, the King of this country, is dead, and now you have got to come and be King."

"Yes, please, sir," said Lionel, "when does it begin?"

"You will be crowned this afternoon," said the other grave gentleman.

The gentlemen led the way to the coach with eight white horses, which stood in front of the house where Lionel lived. And off went Lionel to be made a King.

As the coach went through the town, the streets were all fluttering with flags; there were scarlet soldiers everywhere along the pavement, and all the bells of all the churches ringing like mad, and thousands of people shouting, "Long live Lionel! Long live our little King!"

"I thought this was a Republic," said Lionel. "I'm sure there hasn't been a King for some time."

"Sire, your great-great-great-great-great-grandfather's death happened when my grandfather was a little boy," said the Prime Minister. "But since then, your loyal people have been saving up to buy you a crown."

"But hadn't my great-great-however-much-grandfather a crown?"

"Yes, but he had it made into tin for fear of vanity, and he had all the jewels taken out and sold them to buy books. He was a very good King, but he had his faults. He was fond of books."

Just then the carriage stopped and Lionel was taken out of the carriage to be crowned. Being crowned is much more tiring than you would suppose. By the time it was over, he was quite worn out and was very glad to get into the Palace nursery.

Nurse was there, and tea was ready—seedy cake and plum cake and jam and hot buttered toast and the prettiest china with blue flowers on it and real tea.

After tea, Lionel went down into the library. The Prime Minister and the Chancellor were there, and when Lionel came in they bowed very low.

Lionel cried out, "Oh, what wonderful books! I shall read them all!"

"If I might advise Your Majesty," said the Prime Minister, "I should not read these books. Your great-great-great—"

"Yes?" asked Lionel quickly.

"He was a very good King, but he was a wizard. And you mustn't touch his books."

"Just this one," cried Lionel, laying his hands on the cover of a great brown book. It had gold patterns on the brown leather and gold clasps with turquoise and rubies. And on the spine in big letters he read, *The Book of Beasts*.

The Chancellor said, "Don't be a silly little King."

But Lionel had unfastened the gold clasps, and he opened the book to the first page. There was a beautiful Butterfly all red and brown and yellow and blue, so beautifully painted that it looked as if it were alive.

And, indeed, the beautiful Butterfly fluttered its many-colored wings on the yellow old page of the book and flew up and out of the window.

"Well," said the Prime Minister, "that's magic, it is!"

But the King had already turned the next page, and there was a shining bird complete and beautiful in every blue feather of him. Under him was written, "Blue Bird of Paradise," and all of a sudden the Blue Bird flapped his wings on the yellow page and flew out of the book.

The Prime Minister snatched the book away from the King and shut it on the blank page where the bird had been and put it on a very high shelf.

"You're a naughty, disobedient little King," said the Chancellor.

"I don't see that I've done any harm," said Lionel.

But when Lionel was in bed, he could not sleep for thinking of the book. And when the full moon was shining with all its might, he got up and crept down to the library and climbed up and got *The Book of Beasts*.

He took it outside onto the terrace, where the moonlight was bright. He opened the book and saw the empty pages with "Butterfly" and "Blue Bird of Paradise" underneath, and then he turned to the next page. There was some sort of red thing sitting under a palm tree, and under it was written, "Dragon." The King shut the book rather quickly and went back to bed.

But the next day he wanted another look, so he got the book out into the garden, and when he undid the gold clasps, the book opened all by itself at the picture with "Dragon" underneath, and the sun shone full on the page. And then, quite suddenly, a big red Dragon came out of the book and spread his great scarlet wings and flew away to the far hills.

And then Lionel felt bad. He had not been King for twenty-four hours and already he had let loose a Dragon to worry his faithful subjects. And they had been saving up so long to buy him a crown! Lionel began to cry.

Then the Chancellor and the Prime Minister and Nurse all came running to see what was the matter.

Lionel, in floods of tears, said, "It's a red Dragon and it's gone flying away to the hills and I am so sorry!"

The Prime Minister and the Chancellor had already hurried off to consult the police and see what could be done.

But Nurse did not neglect her duty. She sent Lionel to bed without his tea. "You are a naughty little King," she said. She would not give him a candle to read by.

Next day the Dragon was still quiet, though Lionel's subjects could see the redness of the Dragon shining through the green trees quite plainly.

Now the next day was Saturday. And in the afternoon the Dragon suddenly swooped down and carried off the Football Players, umpires, goalposts, football, and all.

Then the people were very angry indeed, and they said, "After saving up all these years to get his crown and everything!"

Lionel did his best to be a good King during the week, and the people were beginning to forgive him for letting the Dragon out of the book.

All the same, Parliament met to consider the Dragon. But unfortunately the Dragon, who had only been asleep, woke up and decided to eat the Parliament. Every member.

When the next Saturday came round, everyone was a little nervous, but the Dragon was pretty quiet that day and only ate an Orphanage.

Lionel was very, very unhappy. It was his disobedience that had brought this trouble on the Parliament and the Orphanage and the Football Players, and he felt that it was his duty to do something. The question was, what?

The Blue Bird that had come out of the book used to sing very nicely in the Palace rose garden, and the Butterfly would perch on Lionel's shoulder when he walked among the tall lilies: so Lionel saw that all the creatures in *The Book of Beasts* could not be wicked, like the Dragon, and he thought, Suppose I could get another beast out who would fight the Dragon?

So he took *The Book of Beasts* out into the rose garden and opened the page next to the one where the Dragon had been, just a tiny bit to see what the name was. He could only see "cora," but he felt the middle of the page swelling up thick with the creature that was trying to come out. It was only by putting the book down and sitting on it that he managed to get it shut, fastened the clasps with rubies and turquoise in them, and sent for the Chancellor.

"What animal ends in 'cora'?" asked Lionel.

The Chancellor answered, "The Manticora, of course."

"What is he like?" asked the King.

"He is the sworn enemy of Dragons," said the Chancellor. "He is yellow, with the body of a lion and the face of a man. I wish we had a few Manticoras here now. But the last one died hundreds of years ago!"

Then the King ran and opened the book at the page that had "cora" on it, and there was the picture of a creature all yellow, with a lion's body and a man's face, just as the Chancellor had said. And under the picture was written, "Manticora."

And in a few minutes the Manticora came sleepily out of the book, rubbing its eyes with its hands and mewing piteously. It seemed very stupid. And when Lionel gave it a push and said, "Go along and fight the Dragon," it put its tail between its legs and ran away. It went and hid behind the Town Hall, and at night, when the people were asleep, it went round and ate all the cats in town.

And when it had finished, the Dragon came down the street looking for the Manticora. The poor hunted creature, who was not at all the Dragon-fighting kind, took refuge in the Post Office, and there the Dragon found it trying to conceal itself among the ten o'clock mail. And, presently, the people whose windows looked that way saw the Dragon come walking down the steps of the Post Office spitting fire and smoke, together with tufts of Manticora fur and fragments of the morning's mail.

The Dragon was a perfect nuisance for the whole of Saturday.

At last came a day when the Dragon actually walked into the Royal Nursery and carried off the King's own pet Rocking Horse. Then the King cried for six days. On the seventh day, he stopped.

"Nurse," he said, "wipe my face. I am not going to cry any more. I must try to save my people."

"Well, if you must, you must. But don't tear your clothes or get your feet wet."

So off he went.

The Blue Bird sang more sweetly than ever and the Butterfly shone more brightly, as Lionel once more carried *The Book of Beasts* out into the rose garden and opened it very quickly so he wouldn't have time to change his mind. The book fell open wide, almost in the middle, and there was written at the bottom of the page, "Hippogriff," and before Lionel had time to see what the picture was, there was a fluttering of great wings and a stamping of hooves and a sweet, soft, friendly neighing. There came out of the book a beautiful white horse with a long, long white mane and a long, long white tail, and he had great wings like swans' wings and the softest, kindest eyes in the world.

The Hippogriff rubbed its silky-soft, milky-white nose against the little King's shoulder, and the little King thought, But for the wings, you are very like my poor, dear, lost Rocking Horse. And the Blue Bird's song was very loud and sweet.

Then suddenly the King saw coming through the sky the great, sprawling shape of the Dragon. And he knew at once what he must do. He caught up *The Book of Beasts* and jumped on the back of the gentle, beautiful Hippogriff and, leaning down, he whispered in the white ear,

"Fly, dear Hippogriff, fly your very fastest to the Pebbly Waste."

And when the Dragon saw them start, he turned and flew after them, with his great wings flapping like clouds at sunset, and the Hippogriff's wide wings were snowy as clouds at the moon-rising.

When the people in town saw the Dragon fly off after the Hippogriff and the King, they all came out of their houses to look.

But the Dragon could not catch the Hippogriff. The red wings were bigger than the white ones, but they were not as strong, and so the white-winged horse flew away and away and away, with the Dragon pursuing, till he reached the very middle of the Pebbly Waste.

Now, the Pebbly Waste is just like the part of the seashore where there is no sand—all round, loose, shifting stones, and there is no grass there and no tree within a hundred miles of it.

Lionel jumped off the white horse's back in the very middle of the Pebbly Waste, and he hurriedly unclasped *The Book of Beasts* and laid it open on the pebbles. Then he clattered among the pebbles in his haste to get back onto his white horse and had just jumped on when up came the Dragon. He was flying very feebly and looking round everywhere for shade, for it was just on the stroke of twelve, the sun was shining like a gold coin in the blue sky, and there was not a tree for a hundred miles.

It was then that the Dragon saw *The Book of Beasts* lying on the pebbles, open at the page with "Dragon" written at the bottom. He looked and looked again, and then the Dragon wriggled himself back into the picture and sat down under the palm tree, and the page was a little singed as he went in.

As soon as Lionel saw that the Dragon had really gone back into the book, he jumped off his horse and shut the book with a bang.

"Oh, hurrah!" he cried.

And he fastened the book very tight with the turquoise and ruby clasps.

"Oh, my precious Hippogriff," he cried, "you are the bravest!"

"Hush," whispered the Hippogriff modestly. "Don't you see that we are not alone?"

And indeed there was quite a crowd round them on the Pebbly Waste: the Parliament and the Football Players and the Orphanage and the Manticora and the Rocking Horse and everyone else who had been eaten by the Dragon. You see, it was impossible for the Dragon to take them into the book with him. It was a tight fit for even one Dragon.

So they all got home somehow and all lived happily ever after.

Hippogriff

When the King asked the Manticora where he would like to live, he begged to go back into the book. "I do not care for public life," he said. So he got back into his picture and has never come out since.

Then the Rocking Horse begged to go and live on the Hippogriff's page of the book. "I should like," he said, "to live somewhere where Dragons can't get at me."

So the beautiful white-winged Hippogriff showed him the way in, and there he stayed.

As for the Hippogriff, he accepted the position of the King's Own Rocking Horse, a situation left vacant by the retirement of the wooden one. And the Blue Bird and the Butterfly sing and flutter among the lilies and roses of the Palace garden to this very day.

The End